good deed rain

# 44 Books by Allen Frost

...Ohio Trio...Bowl of Water...
...Another Life...Home Recordings...
...The Mermaid Translation...The Selected
Correspondence of Kenneth Patchen...
...The Wonderful Stupid Man...
...Saint Lemonade...Playground...Roosevelt...
...5 Novels...The Sylvan Moore Show...
...Town in a Cloud...A Flutter of Birds
Passing Through Heaven: A Tribute to Robert
Sund.......At the Edge of America.......
....Lake Erie Submarine....The Book of Ticks....
.........I Can Only Imagine.........
...The Orphanage of Abandoned Teenagers...
...Different Planet...Go With the Flow: A
Tribute to Clyde Sanborn...Homeless Sutra...
..The Lake Walker..A Hundred Dreams Ago..
....Almost Animals....The Robotic Age....
....Kennedy....Fable....Elbows & Knees:
Essays and Plays....The Last Paper Stars....
...Walt Amherst is Awake...When You Smile
You Let in Light....Pinocchio in America....
....Florida....Blue Anthem Wailing....
...The Welfare Office...Island Air...
...Imaginary Someone...Violet of the Silent
Movies....The Tin Can Telephone....
....Heaven Crayon....Old Salt....
...A Field of Cabbages...River Road...

# RIVER ROAD

*RIVER ROAD* © 2020
Allen Frost, Good Deed Rain
Bellingham, Washington
ISBN 978-1-64764-426-0

Writing & Drawings: Allen Frost
Cover Print: Julia McIntyre
Cover Production: Jen Armitage
Quotes from:
Charles Beaumont, *Perchance to Dream*, Penguin Classics, New York, 2015.
*From Hell It Came*, Allied Artists, 1957.
D.H. Lawrence from *Studies in Classic American Literature*, "Edgar Allan Poe," Thomas Seltzer Inc., New York, 1923.
Chapter 13 features Fairhaven historical markers.
Apple: TFK!

Moonlight comes fast to small towns near rivers.

—Charles Beaumont

"American magic is better."

—*From Hell It Came*

# RIVER ROAD

Allen Frost

Good Deed Rain ◊ Bellingham, Washington ◊ 2020

There are terrible spirits, ghosts, in the air of America.

—D.H. Lawrence

# CONTENTS

# 1.

A warm day in June. Swallows circled above an overgrown field. A big breath of coal boiled from a stopped train. Underneath that cloud a couple railmen were unloading a coffin. Someone in the boxcar threw a suitcase and a carpetbag next to it. The train whistled. The men jumped back on ladders as the wheels began to move. In those days trains were like dragons. This one roared and it shuddered from the ground where it left its strange cargo, charred through the air, beating the rails, stirring up a hot wind into distant plains. The swallows flew back and forth. The black dust in the air got lost in the breeze. It left the ground covered with a black snow so fine you'd need a telescope to see it. Insects chirred in the weeds and wildflowers rang brightly from the tending of bees. A dragonfly landed on the pine box. A boy would be by later in the moonlight to collect it. That boy will be me. This is a true story, as best as I can remember it. It was the summer I got my first job.

# 2.

I crawled over the windowsill, through the curtains. I could hear a train many blocks away as it yelled its way into town. My hands felt the pebbled roof shingles and spread wide as lily pads while I pulled the rest of me carefully out onto the slant. The chestnut tree above me had a thousand leaves, all applauding, rustling quietly in the breeze. The house underneath my sneakers crackled like whale skin.

# 3.

Robbie Stilvers got me the job. I have him to thank for delivering newspapers at midnight. I didn't have to take the job, but if I didn't, none of this story would exist. Who knows how my life would have changed? Maybe that's why I chose to spend three of my summer nights working for *The Herald, Night Edition.* I knew it would be an adventure I wouldn't forget.

bits of the moon

# 4.

Robbie told me where the pickup truck would be: across a few yards and the baseball field and to the end of Mill Road. He gave me a cloth canvas newspaper bag. He made sure I understood I couldn't do the job without it: I had to bring it with me. I promised I would. I had the strap over my shoulder as I set out that night. There was supposed to be a meteor shower but I only saw two. The gravel in the parking lot shined like broken bits of the moon, the tall sodium streetlights were on. Moths surrounded the glow and if you stood patiently long enough, you could see a bat.

# 5.

The first night of my job I was nervous and I didn't take my time looking for bats and falling stars. Robbie said to get there on time so I took every shortcut I knew. Night eyes getting used to the dark, buttercups balled up fists. A dog barked at the sound of me brushing through the tall black weeds. Another dog barked further away. Beyond that dog would be another one and the story would carry on across to the forested hills. I was their version of the night edition news.

# 6.

Mr. Mose was waiting for me in a dark turn-around off the side of Mill Road. He smoked a cigarette while he stood by the back of his truck. As I came out of the brush he looked at me with smoke coming out of his mouth. "You the boy Robbie sent?"

I said, "Yes sir. I'm subbing for three nights." I saw a stack of newspapers beside him and I wondered how on earth I was going to carry that.

# 7.

It's funny to remember a moment like that now. Mr. Mose stuffed the papers into my shoulder bag for me and the way he handed it over to me, cigarette tipped in his twisted mouth, I thought it would take all my strength to lift. Nothing has ever seemed lighter since then. That's when I knew I was entering another world.

# 8.

    I would soon be learning a lot about the mystery around me and how the eye can be tricked, like how a strongman would lift a heavy looking weight that was really light as a couple balloons. That's how those newspapers were for me. It was circus magic. I slung them to my shoulder like an angel putting on wings.

# 9.

Mr. Mose told me all I had to do. It seemed simple but when he sent me off in the direction of the dark, and what he called River Road, I had to ask to make sure.

"There's nothing there," I said. I've been down that way before. "It's only a wild bit of land."

He said, "You don't know it when the moon is out on a night like this and you have a job to do. Now go."

All I did was follow orders when I was young. If I stopped to think about it I would have been an older man.

# 10.

River Road isn't much more than a lane. When the tar of Mill Road ran out it became a dirt path. Trees crowded in and reached overhead to block out the stars. Who was I supposed to deliver all these newspapers to? It got darker around me. The leaves were moaning like a mummy on a ladder. I wondered if these weightless newspaper shrouds were meant to be left in a hidden cemetery. Would I be surrounded by ghosts with subscriptions to the *Herald*?

# 11.

Pretty soon I was thinking about Sleepy Hollow and the Headless Horseman who used to ride back and forth on a path like this. I listened for hooves. I watched for that faint orange glow of his pumpkin snarl. If he tried to throw it at me, I needed time to leap into the nearest salmonberry bush.

# 12.

The key to being lost is to stay calm. Worry makes it worse. I didn't see much of the path anymore. Branches on either side were tugging at me. For a second I thought I heard music ahead. It only stung the air then it was quiet again. One time I rode out here on my bicycle. I got the same spooky feeling, and that was in the daytime. Our town has a history and there are places like this all around where something left an imprint. Some of them have markers set in the sidewalk, with the details carved into the stone like reminders in a graveyard.

# 13.

HERE IS WHERE
MATTHEW WAS CUT IN
TWO BY A STREETCAR
1891


SITE OF
CITY DROWNING POOL
DOGS ONLY
1899


CHINESE DEADLINE
NO CHINESE ALLOWED
BEYOND THIS POINT
1898-1903


SITE OF
FIRE WAGON AND
HAY BARN
1904

LOCATION OF
TOWN PILLORY
1890


US PRESIDENT
MCKINLEY
BUGGIED PAST HERE
1901


SITE OF
HORSE STABLES AND
CARRIAGE SHEDS
1890


CITY GARBAGE DUMP SITE
"SMELLS LIKE THE BREATH
OF AN ELEPHANT"
1890


HUGE FREIGHT WAGON
DISAPPEARED BENEATH
QUICKSAND HERE
1890

CLEOPATRA'S BARGE
LIONS AND CAMELS
PARADED HERE
1891


SITE OF
STAGECOACH
STATION
1908


SITE OF
CHINESE BUNK HOUSE
CIRCA 1913


SITE OF
SAM LOW'S
OPIUM DEN
1904


SITE OF
CITY POLICE COURT
1909

SITE OF
INTERURBAN
DEPOT
1912-1928


JUNCTION SALOON
NOTHING OF INTEREST
HAPPENED HERE
MARCH 17, 1893


LOCATION OF
TOWN MARSHAL'S OFFICE
1890


TONTINE SALOON
SPIDER BILES NABBED HERE
OCT 1, 1892


SITE OF
APOLLO THEATER
CIRCA 1912

# Crisp, Fresh Green Beans

- U.S. No. 1
- Great raw or cooked!

# 89¢ lb.

thick as pond weed

# 14.

Walking in the nighttime woods I couldn't have read any words like those in the dark but I know something happened here, around the same spot where my bicycle stopped that day. With the spokes tangled up in grass thick as pond weed I had to heave the bike wheel to get out. It felt like I was stuck in the grass of the Sargasso Sea, where ships would be captured forever.

# 15.

I swung my newspaper bag over onto my back and pretended it was a parachute. If I needed to, I could pull the cord and float out of here.

Plenty of leaves and branches and weeds taller than me tried to crowd out the sight of what lay ahead—a ghostly milky light. The spooky feeling hadn't changed. I knew this was one of those haunted places but I had all those newspapers to deliver, and this was where Mr. Mose told me to bring them.

# 16.

As soon as I broke through, the road was back under my feet, packed hard like dirt. It led straight into a neighborhood street, with houses, cars parked underneath trees, gardens and deep pools of shadow. That ghostly light I had seen made everything shimmer. It spun like a nickel. It prickled my skin. It was like one of those gray mornings you could smell the ocean and even though it was a mile away you could feel it on you faint as electricity. I turned my newspaper bag from my back and chose my first *Herald*.

inside a cloud

# 17.

I soon got used to the place. I was inside it now the way you could be inside a cloud. And I was fast as lightning, taking a paper, rolling it tight as a cigarette, with a rubber band in the middle, and then tossing it towards the door of each house. Back and forth across River Road, I was making my way, making good time. I was a natural at being a paperboy. Even when one of my throws went wide and landed in a bush I was quick to untangle it and bring it to the steps where it belonged.

The moon was so big and bright I couldn't tell for sure if it was day or night. That could have been the sun in the sky. It didn't seem to matter. Whatever it was, I could see just fine.

# 18.

At the last house on River Road I had two *Heralds* left. I put one on the doorstep and it took me a minute to guess where the second one went. I put it next to the red painted doghouse beside the picket fence. It was hard to believe I was done. I stood in the gray blue rippling lawn, mesmerized, like watching the TV before bedtime when you're tired and the watery black and white glow fills the darkened room like a swimming pool.

# 19.

River Road ended with that last house. I balanced on the curb. Ahead, a moonlit field full of cabbages spread. There were thousands of them. I could almost hear them sing, softly enough to keep the houses behind me sound asleep. I heard a train on the way and I saw it rush across the distance from right to left. What a lot of noise it made. Even from where I stood it wanted everyone to know a train can march into a room like thunder. It took a while to get quiet enough again to hear the wind in the leaves and the lullaby of the cabbage choir.

# 20.

When I think about it now, I realize what a rare night that was. I didn't know at the time how uncommon it was or where it was taking me, still taking me. I was locked to a signal I believe has never stopped.

I started out across the field, letting River Road become the crumbled soil between two long cabbage rows.

# 21.

If the cabbage field had turned into a lake it would make sense to see someone ahead of me sitting in a rowboat, drifting, maybe with a fishing line in the water. That's what the silhouette told me it was. But we were far from the river and the sea was in the other direction and this crop was no place for a boat. It's true I had no reason to be exploring anymore, I could have hurried back home through the cobweb light, if only I wasn't born with the curious nature to see each mystery as part of a bigger movie I was starring in.

# 22.

As I approached the end of the field, I was still spinning my story. A captain from a torpedoed steamship was taking the train to the capitol. He wasn't seated by a window or in the dining carriage like other passengers. Instead, he was riding in his lifeboat in the baggage car. The sliding doors were open for the breeze, reminding him pleasantly of the ocean's gale. Everything was fine until the train reached this field a short while ago. That's where a dip in the trestle caused the boat to fly airborne, tossed onto the cabbages passing by. There he stood in front of me, wobbled unsteadily. I know it takes a while for sailors to get their shore legs. This wasn't that story though. I could tell he wasn't in a boat. He wasn't in a sailor's uniform. He wore a cape. He seemed to be breathing in the moon.

# 23.

It reminded me of a butterfly starting its life, how he stood with his arms half out, cape limp as new unfolded wings. He wasn't ready to fly but he was thinking about it.

Until I appeared.

I already walked through a ghost neighborhood to get here. Being scared didn't enter my mind. I suppose it should have.

His arms dropped and he said, "Hello." I actually saw that word hang in the air.

I said, "Sorry, I'm all out of newspapers."

He laughed. That didn't matter. With the slow grace of a heron, he stepped out of his coffin.

# 24.

The lid of the coffin closed by itself and the gold letters of a name were illuminated by the moon.

"Are you Count Dracula?" I asked.

"I am Count Misfit," he corrected me. "I have been banished to this land." He swept his cape at the midnight field and pointed at the phosphorous street beyond. "Will you lend me a hand with my bags?"

"Sure." He only had two. A suitcase and a ragged carpetbag. I wasn't sure how he would manage lifting the coffin alone but it rose obediently into the air at his command. He probably could have stood on it and surfed beside me.

banished to this land

# 25.

At the vapory lit edge of River Road's little lane of houses we stopped beneath the tall trees beside a barn. Count Misfit left his coffin hovering and went to check the door. I watched the padlock unclasp and drop easily onto his hand. He wagged his other hand and the coffin drove ahead, leaving a cold wake next to me.

Then Count Misfit looked my way and his eyes were made of silver. He beckoned me and I followed too.

# 26.

Inside the barn a few light bulbs strung from the rafters spaced apart like burning comets and the tall shadow of Count Misfit heaved at a door in the floor. I smelled hay and a cow or two must have been somewhere hiding from the scratch of that medieval trapdoor. I watched him descend into the black underground. I was a bellhop in Transylvania holding onto handles holding who knows what a vampire travels with.

# 27.

I didn't go down there. I didn't have to. I stood aside and watched the coffin tip itself in after him. The two bags I carried tugged out of my grip and scurried across the floor and dropped out of sight. What was I supposed to do? Nothing I guess.

I gave him a minute to get settled in that deep pool, imagining him arranging cobwebs and shadows like a florist, making it picture perfect as the cover of *Crypt Monthly*. What I didn't expect him to be creating in that cavern underground was a radio station.

# 28.

Count Misfit held a small wooden box. It could have been made from a crate of poisoned apples or the slats of a shipwreck. "Thank you for your help," he told me. "I will be safe from the sunlight tomorrow. It's good to have a friend in this world." He handed me the box, "This is for you."

Part of me wanted to say, "Um, no thanks." For all I knew it held the beating heart of a plesiosaur.

He said, "I found this present yesterday in a logging pond."

The box was heavier than I thought it would be, like a bowling ball.

He warned me, "Careful, Thurman."

I was. I opened the lid.

the water at midnight

# 29.

The box held a glass canning jar. Something inside swam in a circle. I said, "What is it?"

"A pollywog dog."

"I never heard of that."

Count Misfit looked surprised. "You mean you've never looked in the water at midnight and waited for one to appear?"

It looked like a regular tadpole but its back legs weren't a frog's. And it had a dog's tail wagging back and forth.

Count Misfit gave me directions to care for the pollywog dog and told me that it would gradually change day after day into an everyday looking dog.

# 30.

I put the jar in my empty newspaper bag. I left the barn and followed River Road. Nobody appeared in the windows but every *Herald* had been retrieved. Whoever lived in those houses was afraid of being seen by the paperboy.

Soon I was through the ghost light and the path lost me in the woods. Oh, I didn't mention the bird before and how it helped me find my route. It just seemed like part of the scenery. Going back through the woods though, it returned, hopping from branch to branch and chirping the same word over and over. Whatever it was saying seemed urgent. It puttered always a few steps ahead of me. I was like a steamship being led into the harbor by a little cartoon tugboat.

afraid of being seen

# 31.

River Road was back under my feet. Tall tree shadows and stars. After what I went through I wasn't worried about the Headless Horseman—he probably lived in one of those glowing houses. He would be sitting beside his coffee with his *Herald*, the sports section folded over and held close enough to read by pumpkin candlelight.

That was my first time working. Mr. Mose's truck was gone when I reached Mill Road. As I continued on, streetlamps began to appear, sidewalks, yards and shortcuts.

I climbed the tree to our roof and crawled in my window. I don't think anyone knew. I was asleep as soon as I lay down.

# 32.

When I went downstairs the next morning and sat at the table for breakfast, I was surrounded by *Heralds* held up and crackling. It felt like sailing with the Spanish Armada. From behind one said, my mother's voice said, "It sounded like something on the roof last night." My father said, "Yes, I heard that too. I wonder what it could have been." Maybe they knew. I didn't say anything. I had a feeling they wouldn't like the idea of me working a job at midnight in a ghost town where I also met a real life vampire.

faster this way

# 33.

Flying by bicycle I left my neighborhood standing on the pedals, ducking branches that I walked under last night. My job would be a lot faster this way. With my *Herald* bag stuffed in the handlebars basket I would be able to toss papers out one-handed, up one row of houses and down the other, sew up the street and be back home in half the time.

The wheels turned on the dirt where Mr. Mose would be later tonight. I ran over the tracks of his truck. Good. In the light of day I wanted to know if it was real. I steered onto River Road. I wanted to see everything again and make sure it wasn't a dream.

# 34.

It was a bright sunny late morning, already getting warm enough to be one of those TV jungle movies. I should have brought a machete or rode an elephant in here. My bicycle knew when it couldn't take it anymore. The spokes were wrapped in creeper, the pedals frozen with weeds. I pressed it into the leaves off the path. I wasn't sure who else used this overgrown trail—Robbie Stilvers came to mind and I didn't want someone like him finding my bike. So I left it covered over and hoped I would remember where it was. If only a gorilla could stand here and guard it for me.

# 35.

Somewhere in the thicket the bird came to my rescue. By now I knew what its job was and I followed that chirp that meant, "This way!" The bird jumped about impatiently when I stopped to pick huckleberries. I had been waiting all year for them to reappear. I got a couple red ones then the twig beside me shook as the bird landed on it. He was so close I could have let him hop on my finger. He had black and white stripes on his head. All he needed was a little blue uniform like a traffic cop. He scolded me again. "Okay, okay," I said and took a step after him. Following was the only cure for all that chirping.

# 36.

It seemed I should have been able to find the last part of River Road on my own, that I didn't need a newspaper bag or a bird to guide me a hundred feet ahead. I've read magic books though and I know a successful illusion can only happen when you follow the steps exactly. As I staggered out of the forest, I expected to see houses facing each other across a one-lane street. When that didn't happen, it was like no rabbit stuffed in a top hat. The carnival glow was replaced by sunshine. There were spotty patches of a road but the houses were gone—nothing but some chimney remains and foundations, stone pens filled with blackberry and wild flowers.

the carnival glow

# 37.

Welcome to the ghost of a ghost town. I walked what was left of River Road, brittle pavement, gravel, sorrel, went around some trees grown as tall as me. It was dust, a dried up riverbed, what you would expect after a ghost died.

Here's what I can say about that now. After all these years I think I have it figured out: Count Misfit fed me a ghost story. That's what I believed for the longest time. That's a pretty simple way to look at it. It could also be some explainable natural phenomenon like the Aurora lights. I think about it this way—on a summer morning a house casts a slow moving shadow. Come back to the same spot later on in the day and it's gone. Like a planet in orbit, I knew River Road would be restored in this spot when I delivered newspapers that night.

# 38.

The barn had vanished too but I went into the brambles carefully to look for where it was built. A meadow grew behind the houses, full of those yellow flowers that look like dandelions but they aren't. It was a good place to bring my pollywog dog when it could run about the way dogs like to. I wondered what it was doing. I left it on a shelf at home. Books were stacked around its jar to hide it from view.

# KINGO

| 14 | 32 | 49 | 68 | 89 |
|----|----|----|----|-----|
| 2 | 27 | 51 | 66 | 100 |
| 15 | 23 | FREE SPACE | 64 | 98 |
| 12 | 31 | 53 | 61 | 83 |
| 17 | 25 | 58 | 63 | 99 |

7497

the experience I needed

# 39.

Sunday nights on TV we would watch *Murder Conductor*. A train stops in some town or city across America and Shelby Wills has to solve a crime. That show gave me the experience I needed to search the grasses for clues. Shelby Wills also had a bloodhound. That helps. Fortunately, it didn't take me long to rediscover the ruins of Count Misfit's castle. I stepped over the cement where the door belonged. With no walls or roof anymore the sun would cook him like Lon Chaney. That was smart to keep his coffin underground. The trapdoor was where it was supposed to be. A rolled up scroll was waiting for me, tied to the rusted latch. My name was spelled in calligraphy.

# 40.

Thurman,
I hope you are doing well.
Thanks for visiting.
As you can tell, I am taking refuge
but I look forward to seeing you
this evening.
Sincerely,
Count Misfit


p.s. Could you stop by Rex's Radio
Repair and collect my order?
Some important supplies I need.
Thanks in advance.

ALL PURPOSE
MISTER & SPRAYER

16 oz.

some important supplies

# 41.

It's funny how I could go from a vampire's dungeon door to Woolworths diner counter in half an hour. I also had time to stop at the radio shop on the way. The Count had a paper bag held for him at the register. The checker told me he didn't know anyone still used radio tubes. A spool of wire made a sort of bird's nest at the bottom of the bag. I didn't say anything. I wondered if I had been hypnotized by Count Misfit into doing his bidding. The $5 in the paper sack was for my trouble. That's why my next stop was a luncheonette. I'm a sucker for a rootbeer float. I also had a sandwich. I was living it up. This was the sort of place I'd like to bring a girl. Romantic.

my next stop

# 42.

I've been coming to Woolworths for years. We would do our shopping here and then get a stool at the blue formica counter. I even know the cook. Oatmeal Houston wears a white cowboy hat. I watched while he made my sandwich, flipped it on the grill until the bread was golden and just like always he brought it to me personally and greeted me, "Howdy buckaroo." I've always pictured him riding to work on a horse, leaving it reined to a drainpipe in the alley. On his break he would go outside to sing it a song, feed it some long stemmed flowers, and make sure everything was okay. When I couldn't sleep, I would shut my eyes and listen for him patrolling the streets on his horse. He was the perfect person to ask about River Road.

# 43.

Oatmeal Houston looked as if the Dalton Gang just walked out of the sporting goods section. He told me River Road had a terrible history, terrible things were done there. We were all better off forgetting. He didn't want to talk about it. He told me I should never go looking for it. I shouldn't even know the name. He wiped his brow with a napkin and took his spatula back to the kitchen. In silence I finished my rootbeer float and most of my sandwich. It had grown cold. That's how I spent my $5 reward.

# 44.

I looked up steep Governor Road and I thought of the mayor. In the 3rd grade he was cast as mayor in the school play. He looked good in a paper top hat and suit. The name stuck. From then on he got ideas. He had ambition. In middle school he ran for class president. Mayor wasn't good enough, I guess. I used to have one of his buttons. He may have had dreams of even more, seeing his name on flyers, signs on lawns and advertised along the sides of buses, with election night coverage on the radio. He was following footsteps to something big. All his friends voted for him, I did too, but it wasn't enough. The footsteps were only lily pads on a pond and not enough to hold him. After that, he was done running, or so it seemed. A year later his family moved to Governor Road. Under the willow on the corner a lady in a red t-shirt held one hand to a lawnmower while it pulled her wheelchair around.

signs on lawns

# 45.

Turning a leaning copy of *R is for Rocket* like a door, the jar with the pollywog dog reappeared. The strange tadpole bubbled across the surface of the water. It looked hungry. I was glad that Count Misfit gave me a shaker of food for it. I don't think I could go into a pet store and ask for pollywog dog flakes. The shaker was like the salt and pepper ones at Woolworths. As soon as I shook some out, my pet flapped its bushy tail and back and forth it went feasting. What an appetite! One of its new paws splashed free, touching the air. It was slowly growing used to life in the air. I don't care what Oatmeal Houston said—as soon as it's ready, I can't wait to take it running in the field behind River Road.

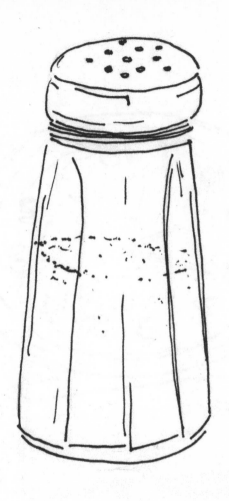

growing used to life

forgetting my job

# 46.

In the summer there seems to be no end to time. With no school, I could do whatever I wished. This day was just the way I wanted it to be and when the end of the day finally reached me I was tired. My alarm was set and pushed under my pillow. Without it to wake me at 11:30, I would sleep on through the night. Nobody in my dreams would remind me I was forgetting my job. I thought for a moment about Count Misfit turned into a bat warning me, knocking on my window with his wing. That was the last I remember until the muffled jangling of my clock. I turned it off and held my breath. The window was open. I heard a train somewhere lost in the stars.

places to be

# 47.

Mr. Mose nodded approvingly, "You got a bicycle."

I coasted up to the truck. Some kids can do tricks, wheelies and stuff. This bike wasn't made for that. It's from Holland. It looks more like an umbrella, spindly black metal, a leather seat, silver spokes and a basket in front.

He asked me how it went last night and was satisfied with my report.

I was looking forward to River Road. The people might still be hiding but Count Misfit was waiting. I had his radio supplies in the basket. I loaded my bag full of *Heralds* and fit it beside the Count's paper sack.

"See you tomorrow," Mr. Mose said. He didn't talk a lot. I've noticed when men get old like him they either talk a lot or not. I prefer the quiet. We both had things to do and places to be. I was ready for River Road.

# 48.

My bicycle track from earlier today left its snake-like scratch ahead of me to follow. Not that I needed a map. I've been tracing my way back and forth enough to be able to sleepwalk it. Once I was slowed down, I left my bike in the usual place. I was surprised there wasn't a parking meter there by now. If this was downtown I'd have to leave a dime. When the woods grabbed hold of me, right on cue I heard chirping and pretty soon I was led safely into the glow.

# 49.

One by one I delivered tonight's *Heralds* and it was the same experience as last time. Nobody showed at the doors, nobody turned a window curtain aside to look. Who was I, the Easter Rabbit? After the last porch and a paper for the doghouse, I headed toward the barn. It loomed like Moby Dick breaking through the luminous. No field or phony dandelions. Someone mowed the lawn and cared for the gardens. A row of watermelons stretched like a bowling ball roll. If I was a pin about to fall down, then far at the end of the lane, past the gutters where the automatic ball return clunks and plastic chairs are gathered around the cluttered table with the score screen, a scarecrow was posed.

# 50.

I haven't heard where scarecrows get their clothes. I've never seen that aisle at Woolworths. It seems they usually wear whatever doesn't fit a person anymore—shirts with holes, jeans that have worn through, hats that have seen better days. The cape was the giveaway. It broke the usual dress code. I hardly had a moment to register who it was before Count Misfit was at my side, faster than rocket powered roller skates.

He wasn't even out of breath. I would be if I slipped across the earth that way.

"Thurman," he smiled. "I knew I could trust you."

# 51.

I watched him climb over that barn easy as a fly, right to the top, trailing wire to where the antenna crowned pointed at the sky. I was just a kid on the ground. If there was more to know, I didn't know it yet.

# 52.

When Count Misfit walked down off the wall I had to ask him about the houses—why did they glow, who lived in them, then in the day where did they go? I had a hundred more questions I could have tacked on. Probably enough to shingle the barn.

He held his open hand towards River Road and explained, "This place is home for the outcasts, cursed to appear and disappear with the moon." His voice sighed away. That wasn't much of an answer either. Count Misfit and Oatmeal Houston should book the Town Hall and give a lecture—*River Road: A History in 15 Seconds.*

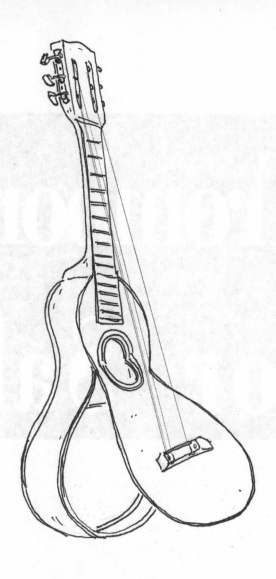

home for the outcasts

# Trombone for Sale

someday perhaps

# 53.

Anyway, his attention turned just like a bat to admire the barn's wired aerial. It made a black spire against the sky. He told me about his underground radio studio and I asked if there a station I could find on the radio dial.

He laughed, "Not yet, Thurman. Someday perhaps. For now you can hear it with this simple device." He had a tin can carried in his cape like a can of peaches. "You will be able to catch the sound with this."

He held it so I could see it was open and empty. Was I supposed to scoop the sound out of the air?

# 54.

Count Misfit attached some wire to the tin can and told me how to tie it to my bicycle handlebars. He said it would be like radio in an automobile. I could pedal along the bank of the river and listen to the sound. But only at night. He said he couldn't step foot in the day and neither could the music.

I know it seems hard to believe that a tin can could pick up a radio signal. Why wouldn't everyone be listening? There were plenty of tin cans around. The city dump would be a symphony.

Count Misfit must have been waiting for me to get back to River Road, to uncover my bicycle, because as soon as I had the tin can attached, it was true—he was right about the music

# 55.

What if I was hypnotized? It wasn't the first time I wondered that. Couldn't vampires do that? Bela Lugosi would glare and poor Lucy would walk out on the rooftops of London like a ghost in a long white veil.

I should have been riding home but I wasn't. I took Marsh Road along the cornfield. I wanted the picture he put in my mind like a Cadillac playing the radio late at night, on the footpath beside the slow flowing moonlit river.

in the morning

# 56.

The birds woke me in the morning. They like the branches of the tree outside my window. The shadow of one flicked across the blue curtain. I looked at my clock and decided I would get up. Good old summer, what a life.

Last night I had to stop before I got home. I took my shoe off and pulled off my sock and stuffed it in the tin can. It was the only way I could think to muffle the sound. There's no OFF button on a tin can. I didn't want to stop listening to that music, but there's no way I could climb into our house blasting the Count Misfit's Show.

# 57.

I had a letter from Count Misfit. He asked if I could do him another favor when he gave me the envelope. In it was a list of records he wanted me to buy and a hundred dollar bill. $100! It was absurd to hold that much cash, like the play money you'd see in a movie. I pedaled with that envelope wrapped in the *Herald* bag, pressed in my basket where I could keep my eye on it. I had to be on alert, I was a target. I was steering an armored car. It had bulletproof glass and two inches of steel. I slowed down at driveways and kept an eye on the road behind me. A sunny hot lazy day squeezed like lemonade but I had to be careful. The next parked car might be full of gangsters.

# 58.

Gangsters didn't hop me over the curb, Mary Isaacs did. It's been a while since I've seen her. We used to see each other in the school library. She liked books as much as I did. I slid the front wheel into the bike rack and slung that valuable *Herald* bag over my shoulder.

It would be fun to surprise her.

The town library had air-conditioning. You felt that right away, as if the books were flowing things, bubbled up from an underground spring.

I knew where Mary would be. The Mystery section was over to my left and I knew she would be bringing a stack of them back to a table. She rarely went anywhere without Agatha Christie.

# 59.

"I don't like reading books that don't have a girl character," Mary said.

"That's a good point," I said.

"What are you reading?"

"Oh. It's a bird book. Do you know much about birds?"

"Some. We have a birdfeeder at home. Our cat likes to watch them," she laughed. "You could come over and ask him. He's an expert on birds."

"I just need to know about one. I see it in the woods sometimes." I flipped the pages and the color photographs flew past, slowing down when I reached the finches, stopping on the White-Crowned Sparrow.

an expert on birds

# 60.

I left the library on Shirley Street. Even if I didn't spot Mary and make a detour I would have turned onto Shirley. The gigantic trees that line the library lot have buckled the sidewalk, pushing the cement slabs into crazy peaks. The tree trunks make me think of elephant legs, a herd of them walking through here, tilting the whole street like a carnival ride.

# 61.

The Record Hive was my next stop. A cartoon bumblebee wearing sunglasses was painted on the door. I stepped right into the music that went all day long. Up and down every aisle, every bin and box—45 singles, 78s, Long Playing albums, even Edison cylinders—Count Misfit had a list but he said I should also pick whatever caught my eye. That cartoon bee followed me on the walls, holding a saxophone, or a guitar, crooning into a microphone, or flying along blissfully, hearing the hum of wings on his back with each flower calling him. That's how it felt to me as I carried the heavy stack of wax to the counter like a bee weighed down with pollen.

# 62.

All this going on and I forgot about my pollywog dog! I rode home fast without stopping this time for a library or a girl. My worry for that little magic creature caused me to think of the worst possibilities. It was all my fault, it was too easy to forget it hidden behind books. I was glad I fed it last night but it was oblivious parenting when I left my room this morning—just me in the day-lit world.

I was running a terrible monster movie in my imagination as I leaned my bike on the backyard fence. Up above I could see my bedroom window. At least it wasn't broken open by some creature lusting for revenge.

in my imagination

# 63.

My room was still as the scene poured from a ship in a bottle. I put the Count's records on my dresser and saw what happened to the bookshelf while I was away. Books were scattered on the floor and the jar had toppled, leaving a damp circle on the carpet. Broken glass and paperbacks, "Oh no…" There really had been a shipwreck. Nothing moved but I couldn't believe the quiet. Where was my pet? How was I supposed to call a dog that didn't have a name yet?

# 64.

I used to feel the imaginary world and this so-called reality existing side by side. I could easily believe a dinosaur lived in the woods and River Road was only a bicycle ride away from my house. I kneeled and carefully picked up all the glass and put my books back where they belonged. Everything looked okay. The carpet felt wet but it would dry. There was nothing out of the ordinary.

# 65.

I looked all over my room, a hundred places high and low: anywhere I thought the pollywog dog might be. I couldn't find it. I kept expecting to hear a watery bark and see it run to me. Finally I sat down on the floor by the window. It was open a bit, enough for a dog with lily pad feet to climb up the wallpaper and hop to the tree.

# 66.

I wanted to think the pollywog dog was on the trail to River Road. It would take it the rest of the day to get there if it was small, driving through the brush no bigger than a matchbox car. I hoped it would make it in time. Night was starting to fall. My tin can radio would go on in a while. I had been waiting all day for the dark like a vampire.

# 67.

I was watching from my window as the last swallows clocked out, turning the sky over to the next shift: flapping bats. At first it wasn't that noticeable. They both diligently crisscrossed the yard, only the bats were more clattery. They looked like actors in a silent film, running after Charlie Chaplin.

Then my tin can radio started to play and the night fell into synch—wind and stars, things with wings, shadows and moonlight moving in tune back and forth like piano keys.

# 68.

The music from that tin can was mesmerizing. Songs I never heard before, by people who had more life than anything I ever found on the radio dial. I never knew there was so much hiding from view. I felt its power directed at me. Was anyone else listening? Why the secrecy? Was it unseen on purpose, was it forbidden or dangerous? I thought of Odysseus. When he sailed past the sirens he made his crew seal their ears with beeswax and tie him to the mast. If I had done that, roped myself to something unmovable in my room, would that tin can radio have lured me over the windowsill in the middle of the night to find the source?

# 69.

My radio played as I pedaled. Sometimes when I went under a really big tree the signal would crackle into static but only for a moment. I had the Count's records wrapped safely in my jacket set in the basket. I was careful to avoid any bump or hole in the road that might make them jump. My night-vision was improving. I was seeing with the moon and the faint light of stars and that was enough. I was also staying alert for my pollywog dog. The tall grass whispered by the crumbling tar. I saw other creatures of the night—raccoons, a possum, a coyote who paused to watch me—but no sign of my lost pet. To keep that worry from turning me around to check every trickling irrigation ditch on the edge of all that farmland, I needed that tin can radio to pull me through.

# 70.

"What's that on your bike? A radio?" Mr. Mose held a cigarette near his face. When he breathed on it, he was wearing a reddish mask.

I told him, "It's the Count Misfit Show." I didn't expect him to say anything. As I've explained, he was usually quiet, but he seemed to know what I was talking about. He didn't say he didn't.

I put the kickstand down and my bike swayed like a horse from the shifting weight of all the records on board. I had to stand it in just the right balanced way so it wouldn't fall over while I got my *Heralds* from the back of the truck.

It's strange I don't remember what was written on any of them. I delivered it for three nights but I just folded or rolled them dutifully. What news of the ghost world was I missing?

# 71.

Mr. Mose let me leave my bike. I couldn't trust River Road's condition on a bicycle carrying newspapers and records on my handlebars. It was safer to walk.

The tin can radio played without me as I started out of the lantern light. Mr. Mose asked if Robbie was working tomorrow night.

He was right. This was already my third night, I was only covering for three. Somehow I put that fact out of my mind. No more little bird leading me to a mysterious town and a vampire.

# 72.

Before the White-Crowned Sparrow found me, I was lost. Yes, my eyes were used to the dark and I should have known River Road by now. Tonight was different though. The woods turned and closed around me, the path shriveled, a loose string, then gone. I kept thinking this would be a good time for that bird to return. Where was it?

That reminds me: a few nights ago I was driving south towards Seattle and I was dialing through the radio. I still do that at night, hoping to find the Count Misfit Show. I believe it can happen. I thought I caught it for half a song—on the flats twenty minutes from town, where the ocean breaks into view and carries with it thoughts of the big wide outside world—then it crumbled in the air. The static is just one more forest for it to hide in.

somewhere for the last time

# 73.

The houses on River Road glowed. Knowing you're somewhere for the last time makes you sip at it slowly. Also, I felt a little more fearless. If it was all going to be gone I had nothing to lose. I went closer to each house than I dared to before. Like a ghost I went from door to door, close enough to look in the windows. The rooms inside were furnished and lived in but I didn't see anyone. I could have let myself in and left a newspaper on a stuffed chair. By the third house it dawned on me, the people might be invisible. Breakfast was set around a dining table, food on plates, a coffee urn, pitcher of orange juice. They were waiting for their *Herald*.

# 74.

I was setting foot on a weird comet that would be going back into the depths of outer space again. I only had this chance to visit before it was crumbled as a dream. The newspapers were delivered. My job was done, the barn waited for me in the shadows.

No Count in the melons tonight, no sign of his silhouette, but the antenna on the roof pierced the deep black sky transmitting his message. Without my tin can though, I couldn't hear the show. I was the loudest thing around, especially when I opened the door. The barn hinges were forged in Transylvania.

# 75.

I couldn't find the light switch but it was okay. I remembered the way to Count Misfit's cellar. It was over by the back wall, past the stables where no cows or horses remained. A blood red sign fizzled above the trapdoor: **ON AIR**.

I leaned the stack of records against a post. The floorboards creaked. He must have been aware it was me, trying to be quiet. I didn't want to interrupt. He was stirring the airwaves, spinning one sound on top of another and another the way a magician twirls plates. It was another form of magic, the music of the spheres, sending radio pulses across the night like ripples on a pond.

# 76.

The night was dark as a tuxedo, the houses were slid up the sleeves. I looked back a couple times as the leaves screened out more and more of River Road until it was only one dot. Once I got my telescope that was the sort of star I'd be looking for. My comet. A few more steps and that astronomical light would drift out of sight.

I don't know what Robbie Stilvers thought of this job night after night. I don't know if he missed it on his three days off. I knew I would. I had been to another world that glowed. Where do you find something like that just walking along, going to school or going home? Oh, I guess I've always been looking for that in the commonplace—the library, a lunch counter—but I was going to remember River Road.

# 77.

I tripped on a branch. My night-vision wasn't as good as I thought. I stopped walking and listened. I was halfway to that dirt turnabout where Mr. Mose parked his truck, where my bike was too. I couldn't hear my tin can radio yet. There were fields on either side. Whatever music the Count was playing underground reached through the earth and writhed in the stalks. I didn't feel a breeze moving them—it had to be him.

The *Herald* bag was empty on my shoulder. I wish I could have filled it with some of that glow. I could have kept it for times of doubt, when I might not be sure that River Road was real.

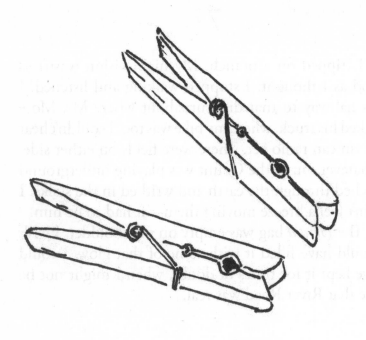

pinned to the air

# 78.

Put ten crickets with tiny violins on my handlebars and that's what I found waiting for me. I thought Mr. Mose stuffed the tin can with straw to keep the volume down. That wasn't it though—my radio was losing its juice.

Off towards the ocean I heard the rumble of thunder. Bigger than the 4th of July, a storm was crawling up out of the water, I could feel the electricity pinned to the air.

I love these summer storms when I'm home in bed, when the window curtain starts to stir. Embers of the hot day cool. While thunder comes on roller skates, getting closer and closer, lightning arrives by streetcar. A Frankenstein switch starts the downpour and the leaves of our tree slash with rain.

I had to climb in my window before that happened out here. I grabbed my bike and pulled it free of the grass and twigs. Riding home racing the wind, the tin can violins were fading, getting smaller than one single cricket whispering into a telephone.

mysteries to see

# 79.

At least I would have a telescope. That's what I thought as I poured myself under the covers, wet as a pollywog dog. When Robbie paid me off and I returned the *Herald* bag, I would go straight to Woolworths, Aisle 11. There were plenty other mysteries to see, River Road was just one of many. I bet I could see fifty of them on the moon.

# 80.

I had a funny dream on my way to Woolworths. Count Misfit sat on a bench in the park. He got caught in the daylight and had turned into a big papier-mâché doll, like something I made in art class. His face was painted on and his clothes were made of tattered newspaper. I picked him up and carried him down Holly Street on our way to River Road. The people on the sidewalk admired my artwork. The envious manikins crowded up to the glass in Woolworths as we walked past.

# 81.

The next morning, sunshine was busy steaming the lawn, birds were singing, flowers turning on, the sort of beautiful July day that would burn Count Misfit into powder. No nighttime satellite competing with other songs for a space in the sky, no more music buzzing in the tin can by my side. I was back to the world I was stuck in three days before. Like a boy on a horse a hundred years ago, I took the *Herald* delivery bag and went for a ride.

# 82.

The river used to have waterwheels to turn and the mills along the wooden banks turned that flow into smoke. It blanketed the town. I imagine it hid the sun from sight. If Count Misfit was here back then he could have leaned on this very bridge rail in daylight, black soot on his hands, while people walked past him in fedoras and there was still a horse or two pulling carts among the cars. If anyone went looking for that past it was only in photographs. So where do they hold onto that world? Where could I look for evidence of River Road? I'll give you a hint—I was there yesterday.

# 83.

The librarian looked in the catalog with me and ran her finger along the words typed on the card. "*River Road*," she said.

"That's it!"

"Historical Fiction," she continued, then, "Oh no…"

"What? What happened?"

"Here," she tapped the handwritten note penciled on the card, "*River Road* is marked as missing."

"Is that the only one?"

"Mmhmm. I'm sorry. It was never replaced either. I'm not sure why. It may not have been checked out enough to be considered necessary."

I sighed, "Oh gee…"

"Do you want me to see if another lending library has a copy?"

I know people shouldn't give up so easily.

# 84.

Leaving the library I was thinking of Mary Isaacs and what she said about a book needing a girl. If I told her about River Road, I bet she would have helped me find out more. She was always solving mysteries.

I didn't see her at the tables, but as I opened the door and left the air-conditioning, she was on her way up the steps. I was glad to see her. I always was.

"Hi Thurman," she said and noticing the *Herald* bag, "Are you a newspaperman now?"

"I was," I admitted, "for a little while." I think I would have explained but I was distracted by someone on the sidewalk below. I recognized the red plaid hunting cap he always wore.

# 85.

Robbie Stilvers was talking to a friend under one of the big trees. His back was to me. His friend—the one with a rattish grin, I forget his name—was laughing and when he saw me I heard him warn, "Here he comes." Robbie turned around and stuck a smile on his face. He lifted his arm, "You got my bag?"

Clutched in my hand, I thought one last time of my chore, filling it with newspapers at the back of Mr. Mose's truck and how it didn't get any heavier with the load. It stayed just as light as when I got it.

something worth more

# 86.

As soon as he had the *Herald* bag, Robbie glanced at his friend then told me, "Sorry, I can't pay you." His friend snorted and stuck a hand over his crooked grin.

"What do you mean?"

Robbie shrugged. "I don't have ten dollars."

What about the telescope, what about the moon?

They laughed.

Now I know it didn't matter. I had seen something worth more than money and a plastic Woolworths' telescope. Those tall trees on Shirley Street didn't try to calm me. They were busy holding up other things, like the sidewalk and the sky.

frozen in time

# 87.

What I did next still surprises me. I guess in that instant I went sort of crazy. I swung my arm out and grabbed that red hunting cap right off of Robbie's head. Why on earth did I do that? His coppery hair, his wide eyes, his surprise, was frozen in time. Then I went running, holding that thing balled in my hand. What a feeling! There are people who seize on to that current and they let it go wherever it pulls them no matter how far or dangerous or mad. I'll admit it was a rush like that river piling under the bridge but I didn't like being swept. I was washed up behind a fence, my back against the warped boards under the scratchy leaves of a willow that made a stage curtain for me. Not one of my finest performances. There was no applause.

# 88.

After a while I got to my feet. I carried that red hunting cap by one of its strings. It swung like a bell, back and forth, calling out for Robbie. I didn't want it. I didn't know what to do with it—keep it for a $10 ransom, tied to a chair, locked in a rental room downtown? I returned to the library taking the long way on Center Street and around the corner to the entrance again. From a distance I saw my bike at the rack where I left it and Robbie sitting alone on the steps, hair shining in the sun, waiting, heaped like the world's saddest robot.

# 89.

"You won't see my money," he told me glumly.

What was I going to do? This wasn't a gangster movie. I gave him the red hunting cap and he became his old self again putting it on.

"Look…" He dug a wallet from his pocket and opened it. It was empty. "Mr. Mose pays me in ghost money. You can't see anything, can you? But it's in there." He removed a thin slice of air and passed it to me. "This is for you."

"What is it?"

"Ten dollars. Don't drop it! Keep it in your pocket."

It might have been another trick—it probably was—something he bought at the magic store—*Fool Your Friends! Invisible Money!*

Robbie watched me bury it in my shirt pocket and told me oh-so-believably, "You won't be able to see it until it's dark tonight."

# 90.

That was the end of our business partnership. And I figured it was the end of River Road. My only remaining connection was a shining tin can radio wired to my bike handlebars. But no music came from it, unless the Count Misfit Show had turned into birds, a barking dog, kids playing in a yard, the hiss of a sprinkler, a passing car, and the leaves high above Shirley Street. I was tuned to it, listening as Mary walked down the steps and greeted me. She held a book against her skirt.

"What would you do," I asked her, "if you had ten dollars that stays invisible in daylight? It can only be seen and spent at night."

She looked thoughtful.

I continued, "I wanted to buy a telescope, but Woolworths is closed by sundown. Most places are."

If anyone could think of the answer, it was her.

# 91.

From time to time I remember my bicycle is a stranger in this land too. How did it travel all the way from Holland to me? In a one-way box stuffed with crumpled pages of *De Telegraaf*. My dad works at the university and he bought it from an exchange student who was going back across the Atlantic without it. How did it feel being abandoned like that? Sometimes when I pedal along, I'll point out the sights of canals and windmills, tulips, paths to the sea worn smooth by wooden shoes. An imaginary Holland only we can see.

# 92.

I was looking forward to the night again. I didn't think that was possible without River Road. Time heals all wounds, or so they say. Once it got dark, I was meeting Mary Isaacs.

I passed the rest of the day looking for the pollywog dog. I tried everyplace I've seen frogs—rain barrels, the pond on Donovan, the swampy ground around the radio tower—and I've gone to the park and checked backyards for dogs. It would help if I knew what it was supposed to look like. I'm assuming it was a dog by now. But maybe it was a rare barking frog? What if it never left our house? Maybe it pitched a tent in our bathtub.

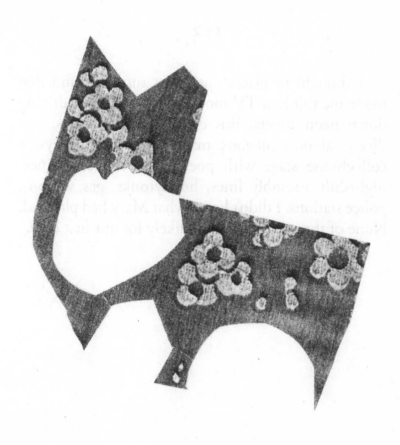

if I knew what it was

# 93.

I thought of places open past sundown and that made me think of TV movies with detectives driving down neon streets. Bus depots, railcar diners, jazz dives, saloons, jukebox machines, pinball alleys, a coffeehouse stage with poetry and modern dance, nightshift assembly lines, honkytonks, gas stations, police stations. I didn't know what Mary had planned. None of those places seemed likely for our first date.

down neon streets

# 94.

I thought of another place we might go and I almost guessed right. The Moonlite Drive In. That was one of the great summer treats of all time. I had seen a lot of movies through the windshield, or when I was smaller from a blanket lying on the hood. What if she arranged for a driver to take us there? Actually, we didn't even need a car: I heard you could sit on the hillside outside the fence. If you brought a radio, you could tune it to the Moonlite station transmitted from the projection booth stilted above the car parked field. The sound of those movies didn't travel much further than the medieval picket wall, but we could listen in that radio shadow and watch with the other kids who didn't have cars.

# 95.

The tall Moonlite projection booth would be the perfect birdhouse for Count Misfit to start his evening prowl. I could imagine him in bat form, skipping across the roofs and hoods of big American cars, flapping into the open window twenty feet in the air, landing on the stacked film cans waiting for him. That's where he would take human shape again, blurred into a long black cape. Cramped in that narrow room he would string the machine with the first reel and when it began to run, pouring out a river of light, he would hypnotize everyone with the vision painted onto the night.

# 96.

At 8:30 PM, I dialed Mary Isaacs. She wrote the numbers on her library book receipt. I had to admire the way she drew them, like birds singing on a telephone wire.

I heard a ring and I waited.

Oh, I should mention another thing—before I called her, I checked my invisible $10. I didn't know if the night had started its magic transformation spell, the dark outside was gradual. Sure enough, when I felt the money and looked at the bill, only half of it was there. The rest still belonged to Mr. Mose, tied and bundled to the *Night Editions* in back of his truck.

"Hello?" Mary said. "This is Miss Marple's residence."

transformation spell

# 97.

If anyone missed me, I left a note in the spotlight beneath my bedside lamp.

I'm not here. It's okay.
I went to see a friend.
I'll be back soon.

Then I crawled out the window...Just another night climbing down the tree. The sun burned bright, low in the leaves, everything painted gold, crows in a tired pale blue sky heading for their roosts. Night turns everything you know into a new world. Nothing is the same, even the bicycle I left by the side of the house. I had to slip quietly, seamlessly from shadow to shadow until I reached the street where I got on my bike and started to pedal.

I know where Mary wanted to meet: it was on the other side of the river. That was pretty clever of her to include herself in spending my magic ten dollars. I couldn't say it aloud but I'm glad she did.

# 98.

Before I reached the river, the street went into the flats where no trees grew and the ground became gray as an old nickel. The land was filled with warehouses and chain-link fences, a boxcar left on a train track cracked above the dirt and loose rock, heaps of slag, a whole world of rusting metal flashed by the setting sun. It would be creepy riding back home through here in the pitch black. A battleship graveyard. A giant muddy tear had fallen overboard onto the cement and the shallow water reflected my bicycle as I stopped. No sign of a pollywog dog. No tiny footprints walking in or out.

# 99.

I leaned on the cold handrail and watched the river. I guess I was thirty feet above the sigh. The sun had sunk into the sea and was swimming towards Japan, leaving behind a seared horizon and an empty pearly blue sky. Day was dying but there was no more night music coming from Count Misfit's tin can. I thought of throwing his radio over the rail but I didn't. I kept it. I still have it. There have been times I wanted to put it on my dashboard and go driving into shadows to search across America for the sound of that long lost show. I don't know if he still haunts the night somewhere. I hope so.

# 100.

Mary Isaacs was looking in the window of a pet store. She had her hand on the glass as if it could pass through and pat whatever was on the other side. The traffic light made a red planet in the air so I could cross the street to her. Every moment, it seemed the night was closing in.

"Hi, Mary. Here I am."

"Can you believe all these animals are waiting for someone to find them?"

I could believe it. We're all the same. In the words of Count Misfit, it's good to have a friend. A cat leaned against the glass beneath her hand.

She turned her attention to me. "I bet you're wondering where we're going to go."

I was. I told her so.

She looked past me and waved.

I heard a car start and saw it pull away from the curb. "Who's that?"

"My mom. She dropped me off. I asked her to wait until you showed up."

just in time

# 101.

I wonder where I would be if I had any sense? Mary Isaacs with her mystery books was way ahead of me. The neon marquee of the Avalon Theatre made a halo over her. "This is it!" she smiled.

Of course!

And we were just in time for the 9:30 show. I locked my bike to one of those trees that always stand around sidewalks and I reached in my pocket.

There was just enough still invisible for her to know what I was talking about. A $10 note with a little bite taken out.

# RIVER ROAD

Allen Frost

drawing & writing:

June—July 2020

Illustration from *Another Life* (2007)

# Books by Good Deed Rain

*Saint Lemonade*, Allen Frost, 2014. Two novels illustrated by the author in the manner of the old Big Little Books.

*Playground*, Allen Frost, 2014. Poems collected from seven years of chapbooks.

*Roosevelt*, Allen Frost, 2015. A Pacific Northwest novel set in July, 1942, when a boy and a girl search for a missing elephant. Illustrated throughout by Fred Sodt.

*5 Novels*, Allen Frost, 2015. Novels written over five years, featuring circus giants, clockwork animals, detectives and time travelers.

*The Sylvan Moore Show*, Allen Frost, 2015. A short story omnibus of 193 stories written over 30 years.

*Town in a Cloud*, Allen Frost, 2015. A three part book of poetry, written during the Bellingham rainy seasons of fall, winter, and spring.

*A Flutter of Birds Passing Through Heaven: A Tribute to Robert Sund*, 2016. Edited by Allen Frost and Paul Piper. The story of a legendary Ish River poet & artist.

*At the Edge of America*, Allen Frost, 2016. Two novels in one book blend time travel in a mythical poetic America.

*Lake Erie Submarine*, Allen Frost, 2016. A two week vacation in Ohio inspired these poems, illustrated by the author.

*and Light*, Paul Piper, 2016. Poetry written over three years. Illustrated with watercolors by Penny Piper.

*The Book of Ticks*, Allen Frost, 2017. A giant collection of 8 mysterious adventures featuring Phil Ticks. Illustrated throughout by Aaron Gunderson.

*I Can Only Imagine*, Allen Frost, 2017. Five adventures of love and heartbreak dreamed in an imaginary world. Cover & color illustrations by Annabelle Barrett.

*The Orphanage of Abandoned Teenagers*, Allen Frost, 2017. A fictional guide for teens and their parents. Illustrated by the author.

*In the Valley of Mystic Light: An Oral History of the Skagit Valley Arts Scene*, 2017. Edited by Claire Swedberg & Rita Hupy.

*Different Planet*, Allen Frost, 2017. Four science fiction adventures: reincarnation, robots, talking animals, outer space and clones. Cover & illustrations by Laura Vasyutynska.

*Go with the Flow: A Tribute to Clyde Sanborn*, 2018. Edited by Allen Frost. The life and art of a timeless river poet. In beautiful living color!

*Homeless Sutra*, Allen Frost, 2018. Four stories: Sylvan Moore, a flying monk, a water salesman, and a guardian rabbit.

*The Lake Walker*, Allen Frost 2018. A little novel set in black and white like one of those old European movies about death and life.

*A Hundred Dreams Ago*, Allen Frost, 2018. A winter book of poetry and prose. Illustrated by Aaron Gunderson.

*Almost Animals*, Allen Frost, 2018. A collection of linked stories, thinking about what makes us animals.

*The Robotic Age*, Allen Frost, 2018. A vaudeville magician and his faithful robot track down ghosts. Illustrated throughout by Aaron Gunderson.

*Kennedy*, Allen Frost, 2018. This sequel to *Roosevelt* is a coming-of-age fable set during two weeks in 1962 in a mythical Kennedyland. Illustrated throughout by Fred Sodt.

*Fable*, Allen Frost, 2018. There's something going on in this country and I can best relate it in fable: the parable of the rabbits, a bedtime story, and the diary of our trip to Ohio.

*Elbows & Knees: Essays & Plays*, Allen Frost, 2018. A thrilling collection of writing about some of my favorite subjects, from B-movies to Brautigan.

*The Last Paper Stars*, Allen Frost 2019. A trip back in time to the 20 year old mind of Frankenstein, and two other worlds of the future.

*Walt Amherst is Awake*, Allen Frost, 2019. The dreamlife of an office worker. Illustrated throughout by Aaron Gunderson.

*When You Smile You Let in Light*, Allen Frost, 2019. An atomic love story written by a 23 year old.

*Pinocchio in America*, Allen Frost, 2019. After 82 years buried underground, Pinocchio returns to life behind a car repair shop in America.

*Taking Her Sides on Immortality*, Robert Huff, 2019. The long awaited poetry collection from a local, nationally renowned master of words.

*Florida*, Allen Frost, 2019. Three days in Florida turned into a book of sunshine inspired stories.

*Blue Anthem Wailing*, Allen Frost, 2019. My first novel written in college is an apocalyptic, Old Testament race through American shadows while Amelia Earhart flies overhead.

*The Welfare Office*, Allen Frost, 2019. The animals go in and out of the office, leaving these stories as footprints.

*Island Air*, Allen Frost, 2019. A detective novel featuring haiku, a lost library book and streetsongs.

*Imaginary Someone*, Allen Frost, 2020. A fictional memoir featuring 45 years of inspirations and obstacles in the life of a writer.

*Violet of the Silent Movies*, Allen Frost, 2020. A collection of starry-eyed short story poems, illustrated by the author.

*The Tin Can Telephone*, Allen Frost, 2020. A childhood memory novel set in 1975 Seattle, illustrated by author like a coloring book.

*Heaven Crayon*, Allen Frost, 2020. How *Ohio Trio* would look if printed as a Big Little Book. Illustrated by author.

*Old Salt*, Allen Frost, 2020. Authors of a fake novel get chased by tigers. Illustrations by author.

*A Field of Cabbages*, Allen Frost, 2020. The sequel to *The Robotic Age* finds our heroes in a race against time to save Sunny Jim's ghost. Illustrated by Aaron Gunderson.

*River Road*, Allen Frost, 2020. A paperboy delivers the news to a ghost town. Illustrated by the author.